—MKM—

THE BOY WHO WAS FIRE

Written by Marcus Kahle McCann

Illustrated by Zita Varga

2019

POCKETS OF...
PUBLISHING

Written by Marcus Kahle McCann
Illustrated and designed by Zita Varga

First published in 2019

For the Kitchens
AND the sinks.

ONCE UPON A TIME ON A DRY, OLD HILL; A SMALL FIRE WAS BORN TO A BRIGHT BOLT OF LIGHTNING AND A TALL, BEAUTIFUL TREE.

THE WISE TREE CRADLED THE
YOUNG FIRE IN HER BRANCHES
FOR AS LONG AS SHE COULD,

BUT IT WASN'T LONG BEFORE HE BECAME TOO HUNGRY AND TOO RESTLESS,

AND SHE HAD TO SET HIM DOWN.

AS SOON AS HIS BLAZING FEET
HIT THE GROUND, HE RAN WILD!
AND HE ATE! HE CONSUMED
EVERYTHING, ANYTHING THAT
GOT IN HIS WAY.

DRY LEAVES, TWIGS,
AND EVEN BUSHES.

4

AND WHEN FINALLY
HE STOPPED TO
CATCH HIS BREATH,

5

HE SAW BEHIND
HIM A PATH OF
RUBBLE AND ASH.

NEWS SPREAD FAR AND FAST
ABOUT THE FIRE, HOW HE WAS ON
THE MOVE AND NOTHING COULD
STOP HIM. WHEN THE FORESTS
HEARD, THEY WERE AFRAID.

AND THE NEARBY CITIES

AND TOWNS COWERED AT THE THOUGHT OF THIS WILD, ALL-CONSUMING FIRE. "HE WILL SURELY DESTROY US ALL!" THEY SAID TO THEMSELVES,

"NO ONE WILL BE SPARED!"

WHEN THE YOUNG FIRE HEARD THEIR CRIES, HE RAN AND HID (AS BEST A FIRE CAN HIDE). AND IN HIS HIDING PLACE, HE GREW.

HE GREW BRIGHT LIKE HIS FATHER AND TALL LIKE HIS MOTHER UNTIL HE WAS SO BRIGHT AND SO TALL AND SO HOT THAT HE COULD NO LONGER BE HIDDEN.

SO HE STOOD UP,

AND HE WALKED.

AND ON HIS WALK, HE
FOUND A LONELY HOUSE.
"CAN I COME IN?"
ASKED THE FIRE.

"IF I LET YOU IN,
YOU WILL BURN ME
DOWN," SAID THE
HOUSE.

"NO, NO," SAID THE FIRE, "IF YOU LET ME IN, I WILL BE WARMTH FOR YOU IN THE COLDEST OF WINTERS,

AND I WILL BE LIGHT FOR YOU IN THE DARKEST OF NIGHTS.

AND AS LONG AS I'M ALIVE,
NO BANDIT WILL DARE
TRESPASS UPON YOU."

14

THE HOUSE LOOKED
AT THE FIRE AND WAS
SKEPTICAL,

BUT THEN SHE
SAW THAT
BEHIND HIM

16

GREEN THINGS WERE
GROWING IN HIS FOOTSTEPS,
VERITABLE GARDENS IN THE
PLACES HE'D WALKED.

WHERE ONCE THERE
WERE ONLY DEAD AND
BURNED THINGS, THERE
WAS NOW LIFE!

SO SHE LET HIM IN.
AND HE BURNED IN
THE HEARTH OF
HIS HOME,

AND HE AND THE HOUSE WERE VERY HAPPY.

WHEN THE FORESTS
SAW THAT THE FIRE
HAD FINALLY FOUND
REST, THEY FEARED
NO MORE.

AND IN TIME, THE CITIES
AND TOWNS INCORPORATED
THE HOUSE THAT WAS NO
LONGER LONELY.

AND THE FIRE'S FATHER
FLASHED FROM HEAVEN,
AND HIS MOTHER SMILED
ATOP HER LUSH HILL.

ABOUT THE AUTHOR

Kahle is an award-winning playwright and lyricist and is part of the Mildly Fearsome Films, a production company based in Los Angeles where he lives with his wife, Becky. Kahle firmly believes that if writers write at the top of their intelligence, Readers will read at the top of theirs and that if they read or hear enough stories that are "over their heads," it won't be long before they have taller heads... not literally... Kahle does NOT promote the idea that literacy leads to weird cranial mutations.

ABOUT THE ILLUSTRATOR

Zita is a Hungarian artist and graphic designer, working as a freelancer and living in Prague with her boyfriend, Daniel. Zita believes in the magical power of the visual arts to enlighten, inspire, and empower. If you would like to see more of her work you can do so at zizugraphics.com.

CPSIA information can be obtained
at www.ICGtesting.com
Printed in the USA
LVHW011949250719
625401LV00001B/1/P